To my boys,
Miles and Jack.

ISBN-13: 978-0-9818519-2-1
Fili finds he is one of a kind.

Written By: Annie Ratta

Copyright © 2017 by Annie Ratta
First Edition, 2017

Published By: WordCutter, Sacramento, CA
Published in the United States of America

Deep in the rainforest, the monkey with 7 years at his back sipped from a leaf full of rain from the great Costa Rican sky.

Fili was an adventurous monkey with an entire jungle to explore.

Using his beak, Blue Parrot plucked a feather from his tail...

...and stuck
it in Fili.

You are so blue and now I am blue too! Gracias!

Fili used his new blue tail

to swing from vine to vine,

tree to tree until ...

He surprised a purple snake hanging from a branch!

You are so purple! I am only brown and blue. Can I be purple too?

Purple Snake used her slithering tongue and sucked up a purple scale from her purple tail...

And she spit it on Fili's belly.

I am brown, blue and
now purple too!
Gracias. Adios!

Fili jumped from the tree and slid on his purple

belly along the forest floor until...

...his path was blocked
by a very busy beetle!

You are so orange and I am only purple, brown and blue. Can I be orange too?

Beetle had more than enough to share and plopped one of his orange polka dots from his shell...

...right on Fili's face!

I am brown, purple, blue, and now I am orange too!

Fili continued on happily with his orange face until...

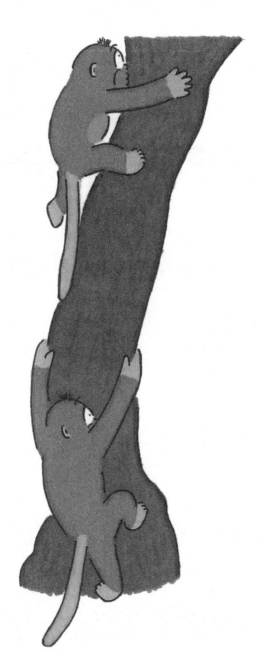

...he came
eye to eye

with a big
Red Sloth!

You are so red and I am only purple,

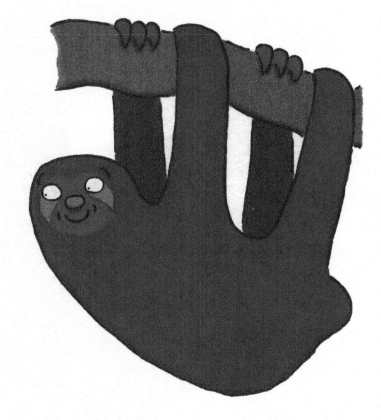

brown, orange and blue. Can I be red too?

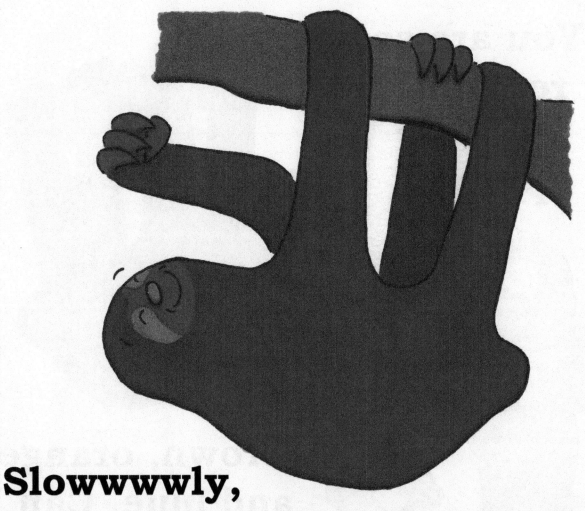

Slowwwwly, slowwwwy, softly, Red Sloth surrendered a red claw.

Red Sloth put it

in Fili's paw.

I am brown,
purple,
orange, blue
and now I am
red too!
Gracias!
Adios!

Suddenly the forest shouted and rain begain to fall. Fili was soon soaking wet. He looked down at his beautiful new colors and was shocked at what he saw!

With every drop, his colors started to blend,

Before he knew it, he was BROWN again!

The rain came and went and
Fili was dry and brown again.
All of his colorful friends
suddenly came out to see the
sunshine through the treetops.

Fili was sad until he noticed purple, red, blue and orange and yet there was no brown.

The forest
needs a
purple, a red,
a blue, an
orange...

...and a brown too!

The forest needs everybody!

Pura Vida!

CPSIA information can be obtained
at www.ICGtesting.com
Printed in the USA
LVOW02*0727020617
536700LV00001B/2/P